Picture Perfect

I wish, I wish
With all my heart
To fly with dragons
In a land apart.

By Alison Inches
Based on the characters by Ron Rodecker
Illustrated by The Thompson Bros.
A Random House PICTUREBACK® Book

Random House 🏠 New York

Text and illustrations copyright © 2002 Sesame Workshop. Dragon Tales logo and characters ™ & © 2002 Sesame Workshop/Columbia TriStar Television Distribution. All rights reserved under International and Pan-American Copyright Conventions. Published in the United States by Random House, Inc., New York, and simultaneously in Canada by Random House of Canada Limited, Toronto, in conjunction with Sesame Workshop. Sesame Workshop and its logos are trademarks and service marks of Sesame Workshop.
Library of Congress Cataloging-in-Publication Data
Inches, Alison. Picture perfect / by Alison Inches ; illustrated by the Thompson Bros.
p. cm.—"Based on the characters by Ron Rodecker." "Dragon tales."
SUMMARY: When Cassie tries to organize the rest of the dragons to help paint a mural on the playground wall, she is disappointed that they are not very enthusiastic about the project. ISBN 0-375-81607-0 (pbk.)
[1. Individuality—Fiction. 2. Painting—Fiction. 3. Magic—Fiction. 4. Schools—Fiction. 5. Dragons—Fiction.]
I. Thompson Brothers Studio, ill. II. Title. PZ7.I355 Pi 2002 [E]—dc21 2001050181
www.randomhouse.com/kids/sesame
Visit Dragon Tales on the Web at www.dragontales.com
Printed in the United States of America   June 2002   10 9 8 7 6 5 4 3 2 1
PICTUREBACK, RANDOM HOUSE, and the Random House colophon are registered trademarks and the
Please Read to Me colophon is a trademark of Random House, Inc.

*S*quish! *Swish! Splat! Sploosh!*

"There!" said Cassie triumphantly to Quetzal. "All done!"

Cassie's dragon friends had asked her to paint a picture of their teacher to hang in the classroom.

"It is a perfect picture!" said Quetzal. "You have a gift for painting, little Cassie."

Quetzal looked thoughtfully at Cassie's painting.
"You know," he said, "we need a mural for the playground wall.
Would you like to be in charge of it, Cassie?"
Cassie clapped her hands. "Oh yes!" she said. "Thank you, Quetzal!"

Cassie could hardly wait to start. "I'm sure everybody will want to help," she told herself.

So Cassie washed the wall and then poured paint into six buckets—one for herself and each of her friends.

Then she picked paintbrushes from the brush that grew in the meadow.

"There!" said Cassie when she had a handful. "Everything's ready!"

Cassie found Max and Emmy on the other side of the
playground and asked them if they wanted to paint.

"I'm a great color-innerer," Max said, "but I'm not so
good at painting. I think I'll play instead."

"Me too," said Emmy. "You like to paint, but I like practicing my soccer moves." Emmy kicked the ball.

"Score!" shouted Max from the jungle gym. "The fans go wild!"

Cassie shrugged. "All right," she said, and went on her way.

Cassie flew over to Ord's house next.

"Do you want to help paint a mural for the School in the Sky playground?" asked Cassie.

"Gee, thanks for asking," said Ord. "But I'm not so good at painting." Ord slipped an apron over his head. "But I *am* good at baking! I was just about to make some rainbow cupcakes."

"Okay." Cassie sighed as she turned to leave. "Thanks anyway."

"I'll save you one!" Ord called after her. "At least, I'll try!"

"Oh, I hope, I hope, I *hope* that Zak and Wheezie want to help," thought Cassie, sliding down their knuckerhole.

"Painting is just not our thing," said Zak. "We're good at playing music, so that's what we like to do."

"Hit it, Zaky!" said Wheezie. They began to bang out a song together as Cassie flew sadly away.

Cassie flew back to the playground, but painting the mural just
didn't seem like much fun anymore. A teardrop splashed onto her toes.
"Little Cassie, what seems to be the trouble?" asked Quetzal.

"Nobody wants to paint the mural with me," Cassie answered, sniffling. "They all want to do other things."

"Well, *niña,* you must do what *you* like to do," said Quetzal, "and then see what happens."

"Well, I guess I can try," said Cassie.

Quetzal handed Cassie a bottle filled with glittery powder. "Sprinkle this in your paint. It will make it *especial,*" he said.

Cassie put on her smock and tipped her beret to one side.
Then she sprinkled Quetzal's special powder into the paint.
"Ooh, sparkles!" she gasped, watching the colors swirl.
Then *Sploosh! Swish! Swish!* Cassie began to paint.

Before long, Cassie discovered that she had an audience.
"What's your picture called?" asked Emmy.
"'Dragon Dance'!" said Cassie.
The moment she finished her picture, the paint began to twinkle and the brush strokes began to move. The dragons in the picture were dancing!

"Whoa!" said Max. "I wish *I* could paint like that!"
"I bet you can!" said Cassie with a happy smile.
She handed him a brush. "Here, give it a try."

Max painted some stick figures. The magical paint sparkled and
swirled and the stick figures turned into Max doing his favorite things.
"See what I did?" said Max. "I'm the best painter in the whole world!"

Ord went next. "I'm good at drawing shapes," he said. He painted a triangle, a square, and a circle.

When the magical paint began to bubble, Ord's shapes changed. . . .

"I see a slice of pizza!" said Cassie.
"And cocoa cake!" said Zak and Wheezie.
"Look! A dragonberry cookie!" cried Max.
"They even *smell* like the real thing!" said Emmy, sniffing.
"*Mmmm,*" said Ord. "Painting makes me hungry!"

"Let me!" said Emmy. She painted a soccer game.
"I knew it!" she cried. "The players really move!"

"We want to try!" said Zak and Wheezie.
Together they splattered the wall with spots. When the magical paint connected the dots, everyone could hear music.
"Loooooove it!" said Wheezie.

When Quetzal came to see the finished picture,
everyone stood back and admired the mural.
"It is picture perfect, *niños*!" Quetzal said.

"Thanks for sharing what I like to do," said Cassie.
"Thanks for letting us try," said Emmy.
"Trying is easy," said Max. He looked around at his friends and giggled. Everyone was splashed with glittery, sparkly paint. "Cleaning up—now *that's* going to be hard!"